W9-AFM-506

Three
Lost Seeds

Text © 2019 by Stephie Morton • Illustrations © 2019 by Nicole Wong • Hardcover ISBN 978-0-88448-764-7 • eBook ISBN 978-0-88448-766-1 • First hardcover printing September 2019 • Tilbury House Publishers • 12 Starr Street • Thomaston, Maine 04861 www.tilburyhouse.com • All rights reserved. No part of this publication may be reproduced or transmitted in any form or by any means, electronic or mechanical, including photocopying, recording, or any information storage or retrieval system, without permission in writing from the publisher. • Library of Congress Control Number: 2019940871 • Designed by Frame25 Productions • Printed in Korea • 15 16 17 18 19 20 XXX 10 9 8 7 6 5 4 3 2 1

Three Lost Seeds

STORIES OF BECOMING

Written by Stephie Morton

Illustrated by Nicole Wong

TILBURY HOUSE PUBLISHERS,
THOMASTON MAINE

Every seed knows
in spring, when it grows,
what plant it is planning to be.

If treated just right,
it will wake in warm light
to burst from the dirt and shout, "ME!"

But some seeds get taken
before they awaken
to places they don't want to go.

With few of their needs met,
these unhappy seeds get
discouraged and struggle to grow.

Still, Nature is smart
and has a big heart
for helping a lost seed be found.

She likes problem-solving,
adapting, evolving,
and turning the trouble around.

This seed in a suit
of sweet cherry fruit
got whisked off inside a bird's beak!

Wild winds during flight
gave the bird such a fright,
he dropped the small seed in a creek.

That's how it got stuck,

deep down in the muck,

unnoticed and barely alive.

When, WHOOSH came a flood

that pushed all the mud

downstream so the seed could survive!

Though tattered and tired,

it now felt inspired

to do what a seed's meant to do.

As soil hugged its skin,

the seed snuggled in

for a long winter's rest. Then it grew.

Once captured by ants,
this seed had no chance
to stay near its own bushland tree.

Brought to the unknown,
in the dark, all alone,
the seed only wished to break free.

Above lightning crashed.

Then wild fire flashed.

Acacia groves set ablaze!

When flames raced through fast,

no green was bypassed.

The trees burned to black and ash grays.

But in the ant nest,
the seed, a plant guest,
was safe and could see what was true.

Its luck had depended
on being befriended
by strangers. Beside them, it grew.

This seed loved to float
in a pod, like a boat,
until the earth started to shake.

Made dizzy, it whirled
while lake water swirled
down crevices caused by a QUAKE!

Left on the dry bed,
it soon laid its head
and fell asleep thirsty but strong,

sure never to quit,
determined that it
would wait there no matter how long.

In time the lake healed.
The crevices sealed,
for Nature tries hard to renew.

When rain filled the crater
ONE HUNDRED YEARS later,
the lotus seed drank up and GREW!

So when you're outside
on a walk or bike ride
and a new seedling catches your sight,

stop. Share a sip.
Ask, "How was your trip?"
Say, "Glad that you made it all right!"

Seeds and Kids: A Note from Stephie

Do you remember planting your first seed in kindergarten? Did you fill a plastic cup with dirt, bury a little bean, water it carefully, and place it in a sunny window? Did you check on it every day until one morning, like magic, a little curled-up stem with a tiny leaf peeked up at you?

Growing is not nearly as easy for a seed outside the classroom. In the wild, seeds can't grow close to their parent plants or they will become too crowded, without enough water, sunlight, or nutrients to go around. In the wild, seeds might not get enough water, or they might get too much. They might not get a bed of soft, rich dirt to germinate in.

It's a good thing Nature is ingenious! Plants have developed a wonderful variety of ways to send their seeds into the world. Seeds can be dispersed by wind, water, animals, or bursting pods. The cherry tree, acacia tree, and lotus plant in this story have different methods of seed dispersal, and all of them are amazing.

The Middle Eastern cherry tree, like its cousins in the rest of Asia, Europe, and North America, surrounds each seed with a sweet, fleshy fruit that birds and mammals carry off to eat. But don't worry: The tree protects the little seed inside the fruit with a shell so tough it can withstand the icky trip through an animal's digestive tract and grow when it comes out the other end! It can survive a flash flood and a fall from a great height, too.

The acacia tree that lives in the hot, dry bushlands of Australia receives little water with which to create a juicy fruit, so instead it encases its hard seeds in long pods and surrounds each one with an oily, sticky, orange tissue (the *elaiosome*) that tastes yummy to an ant. Ants come running, tear open the pods, carry the seeds back to their nest, gobble up the sticky coating, and store the undamaged seeds in a special garbage room. If a flash fire burns the trees, the seeds are safe underground, where they have everything they need to grow and thrive after the fire.

The lotus plant grows in lakes and ponds all over Asia. It spreads its seeds by allowing them to fall off and float away. Lotus seeds have been given a mysterious survival skill—the gift of longevity. Scientists are trying to discover how lotus seeds left in dry lakebeds for hundreds of years are able to come back to life and grow new plants!

These seeds are among the countless numbers that survive hard journeys to thrive in new surroundings. When you think about it, every plant is a miracle. Every child is a miracle too. In my imagination, this story of seeds is like the stories of refugee children who are separated from their families and forced to leave their homes. Like seeds, children thrive when given the chance.

Seeds and Seed Banks

by Dr. Gayle M. Volk

Seeds are amazing vessels whose coats protect plant embryos. Seeds can often be stored and protected under cold, dry conditions for decades or even hundreds of years. Many nations have created seed banks in which seeds are protected for the future. Scientists use the seed banks for research and breeding, and they are available in case disaster strikes and supplies must be replenished. I work at a large seed bank in Fort Collins, Colorado, in which more than 500,000 seed varieties are stored in freezers and liquid nitrogen. My fellow scientists and I research new ways to collect and keep seeds safe for future generations.

It is important to understand where our food comes from and to realize that seeds are critical for human survival. All plants originate from seeds, including those that produce fruits, vegetables, oils, and grains. Third-graders at a Fort Collins elementary school visit the seed bank each year, learning that although seeds come in many shapes and sizes, all have the same basic components and functions. The students gain an understanding of how seeds can be kept cold, dark, and dry for a long, long time—unchanging through all that time—then spring to life in warm, moist conditions.

And the students learn that there is much more diversity in seed banks and in food crops grown around the world than you will find in a local grocery store. A key goal of the program is to demonstrate that agriculture is the discipline that feeds the world.

Three Lost Seeds provides a captivating story to introduce children to the unique magic of seeds.

Dr. Gayle M. Volk is a plant physiologist at the USDA-ARS National Laboratory for Genetic Resources Preservation in Fort Collins, Colorado.

About the Author and Illustrator

Stephie Morton learned many things when she moved to the Colorado mountains with her husband and two young children. She learned she could tolerate a few "helpful" spiders in the cabin but not in the shower. She learned if you pick all the wildflowers in the streambed, they will never pop up there again. And she learned that having fun in nature was all about opening herself up to the wonder. She watched her kids do it instinctively. When hanging out with them, Stephie felt she absorbed wonder like sunshine. Stephie founded a children's art school, Ideas Happen Here, where she has encouraged creative expression for over 30 years. A student once called her classroom "the magic side of the world." Visit her at ideashappenhere.com.

Nicole Wong was raised by a designer/painter dad and a fashion illustrator mom and never thought of becoming anything except an illustrator. She has illustrated twenty children's books using oils, watercolor, ink, and digital media. Visit her at nicole-wong.com.